Making Rea

Chrysalis Childi

Falkirk Council

For Sue Lin

First published in Great Britain in 2005 by
Chrysalis Children's Books
An imprint of Chrysalis Books Group plc
The Chrysalis Building, Bramley Road, London W10 6SP
www.chrysalisbooks.co.uk

Text and illustration copyright © Nick Ward

The moral right of the author has been asserted

A CIP catalogue record for this book is available
from the British Library.

ISBN 1 84458 126 8

Printed in China

2 4 6 8 10 9 7 5 3 1

This book can be ordered direct from the publisher. Please contact
the Marketing Department. But try your bookshop first.

I Wish...

NICK WARD

Chrysalis Children's Books

"I wish," said the little boy
with eyes shut tight,
"I wish I may,
I wish I might..."

Now that it's night time,
my teddy and I,
could open the window
and through it we'd fly...

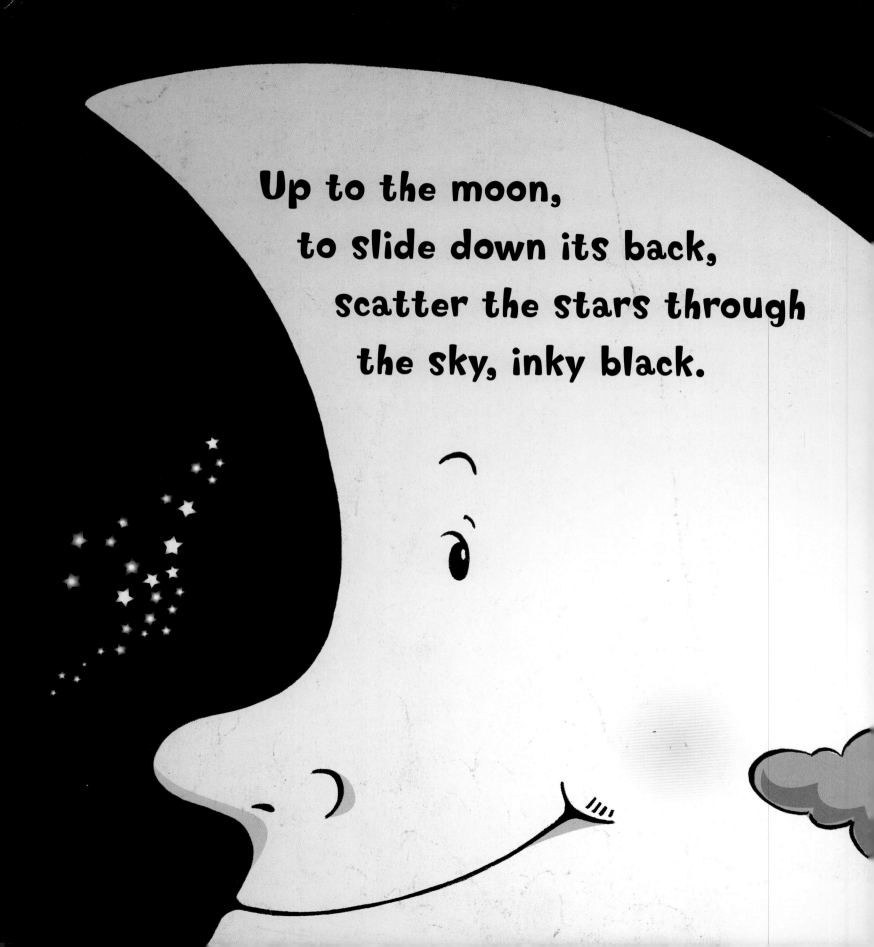

Up to the moon,
to slide down its back,
scatter the stars through
the sky, inky black.

Make them crackle,
then fade and sparkle again,
as we fall through a cloud
and turn on the rain.

Sink under the waves,
leave a silvery trail,
to be lifted at once on
the hump of a whale.

Past galleons laden with
gold we would glide,
as a thousand bright fishes
flashed by our side.

And from a moonlit crag,
narrow and tall,
a lonely mermaid princess
would call.

Our whale would surge through the bubbling foam and sing us his song as we headed for home.

Then as the whale sailed
close to the shore,
Teddy and I would take
flight once more...

Over the rooftops, through silent streets, tap on the windows of the world as it sleeps.

And as the town clock
started to chime,
we would fly on
towards morning time.

As a new morning sun
rose in the sky,
safely in bed with
Teddy I'd lie.

"I wish," said the little boy
with eyes burning bright,
"I wish I may,
I wish I might..."

More fun books for you to read!

ISBN 1 84365 056 8

ISBN 1 84458 140 3 (pb)

ISBN 1 84365 061 4

ISBN 1 84365 026 6 (hb)
ISBN 1 84458 157 8 (pb)

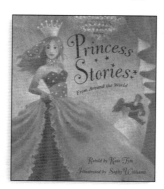

ISBN 1 84365 025 8

ISBN 1 84365 017 7